Gift Aid item

GW00866003

MINI CLASSICS

BRER RABBIT
AND THE
TURTLE RACE
And Other Stories

RETOLD BY STEPHANIE LASLETT
ILLUSTRATED BY STEPHEN HOLMES

THE BOOK COMPANY

TITLES IN SERIES I AND II OF THE MINI CLASSICS INCLUDE:

SERIES I

Aladdin and the Magic Lamp

Ali Baba and the Forty Thieves

Alice in Wonderland

A Child's Garden of Verses

Cinderella

The Emperor's New Clothes

The Frog Prince

Goldilocks and the Three Bears

Hansel and Grettel

The Happy Prince

The Little Mermaid

Mother Goose's Rhymes

The Owl and the Pussycat (and other Nonsense Verse)

Puss in Boots

Sleeping Beauty

Snow White and the Seven Dwarfs

The Town Mouse and the Country Mouse (and other Aesop's Fables)

The Three Little Pigs

The Ugly Duckling

The Wizard of Oz

SERIES II

Beauty and the Beast
Brer Rabbit and Brer Fox
A Christmas Carol
The Hare and the Tortoise
How the Leopard Got His Spots
Jack and the Beanstalk
The Magic Carpet
The Night Before Christmas
Pinocchio
Rapunzel
Red Riding Hood
The Secret Garden
The Selfish Giant
Sinbad the Sailor
The Snow Queen
The Steadfast Tin Soldier
Thumbelina
The Walrus and the Carpenter
The Wind in the Willows I
The Wind in the Willows II

A PARRAGON BOOK

This edition published and distributed in Australia in 1995
THE BOOK COMPANY INTERNATIONAL PTY LTD.
9/9-13 Winbourne Road, Brookvale, Sydney, NSW 2100, Aust

Produced by
The Templar Company plc,
Pippbrook Mill, London Road, Dorking, Surrey RH4 1JE

Copyright © 1995 Parragon Book Service Limited, Bristol, Eng

Designed by Mark Kingsley-Monks

Printed and bound in Great Britain

ISBN 1-85813-800-0

Many years ago on a big cotton plantation down in the deep south of North America there lived an old black slave called Uncle Remus. Every evening as the sun set behind the persimmon trees and the shadows lengthened across the dusty yard, Uncle Remus would sit in a creaky old rocking chair on

5

the verandah, light his pipe
and tell his tales to anyone
who would care to listen. If
the children were good and
quiet then they could listen
too and so they heard all
about the days when
animals strolled around just
the same as us folks.

These are some of those
stories that Uncle Remus
told long ago.

It was springtime and everyone felt mighty glad to be alive. Brer Rabbit felt especially full of the joys of spring as he nibbled the tender, juicy shoots in the peanut patch. He was smart and always the first to find the freshest leaves! But one day he met his match and then he didn't look quite so happy, I can tell you.

One fine spring day as
Brer Rabbit ran lippity
clippity up the road he
passed by old Brer Turtle.

"Good job you ain't in no
particular hurry," scoffed
Brer Rabbit as he raced by.

"I could go as fast as you if
I wanted, *which* I don't,"
replied Brer Turtle, calm as
you please. Brer Rabbit
skidded to a halt and walked
back towards the Turtle.

"Say *what*?" he exclaimed, disbelievingly. "Why, you're so slow that by the time you get to the shops, they've drawn down the shutters, locked the doors and gone home to tea."

Well, before long they fell to arguing about who was the fastest and, blow me, if ole Brer Turtle didn't issue a challenge right there and then.

"I ain't gonna argue the oss no more," says he. "Tucked away out of sight n a chink of my chimney at nome there's a fifty dollar bill says I'll beat you fair and square." Brer Rabbit could not believe his ears. *Easy* money!

"And *I* have fifty dollars says you're gonna kiss my neels, Brer Turtle!" says he, with a delighted grin.

"Why, I could sew grass seeds as I run along and by the time *you* pass that way, they'd be grown tall enough to give you a good meal!"

Well, ole Brer Turtle was having none of it and calmly repeated that he was sure he could beat Brer Rabbit in a race. With a pitying shake of his head, Brer Rabbit agreed to take part in the challenge and so it was all arranged.

Brer Buzzard was summoned to be the judge and Brer Bear was given the important job of firing the starting pistol. A five mile course was measured off with posts to mark the end of every mile. Brer Rabbit was going to run along the road but for some reason Brer Turtle decided he would race through the wood. Folks said he was plumb crazy to choose such a course, but that Brer Turtle, he knew what he was doing, all right.

Brer Rabbit began to train like a professional. He jogged up and down the dusty road for four hours every day. He skipped, he lifted weights, he wore a bright pink track suit and drank fizzy water.

And how did ole Brer Turtle train for the big event? Well, he lay in his swamp and dozed. Now Brer Turtle had a big family. He had a wife and three children, all the spitting image of their father. You could put them under a magnifying glass to tell them apart and even then there'd be no cast iron guarantee you'd get it right.

So Brer Turtle quietly snoozed in the mud and Brer Rabbit pumped iron until his muscles felt ready to pop.

The day of the race dawned clear and bright and even before sun up, Brer Turtle and his family had got themselves into position. Brer Turtle had a plan, a very good plan. He had thought of a way to beat that boastful rabbit and teach him a lesson once and for all. His family had their instructions and knew just what to do. Brer Turtle's wife waited by the starting post, and his three children each waited behind the next three posts, and where was Brer Turtle? Why, hiding in the woods near the very last post of all, of course!

Soon a big crowd had
gathered to watch the race
and Miss Meadows and her
girls were there to cheer
them both on.

Brer Rabbit jogged at the starting line as Brer Buzzard called, "Take your marks!"

"Ready when you are," cried Mrs Turtle and she sounded just exactly like Brer Turtle.

"Ready, steady, go!" cried Brer Bear and they were off! Brer Rabbit raced down the road past the hooting crowd, but ole Mrs Turtle scuttled off into the wood.

Start

27

When Brer Rabbit reached the first mile post he called out, "You there, Brer Turtle?" and Brer Turtle's eldest child crawled out onto the road and said, "Right behind you, Brer Rabbit." Then Brer Rabbit set off again like a steam train and young Master Turtle went home.

Soon Brer Rabbit reached the next mile post.

"You there, Brer Turtle?"
he said. And out crawled
Brer Turtle's middle child.
"Sure am," said she, and
crawled off home. But Brer
Rabbit just carried on
steaming down the road.
 The same thing happened
at the next mile post and
this time Brer Turtle's
youngest little 'un crawled
out, put in an appearance
and went home.

Panting breathlessly, Brer Rabbit loped along the final mile. "Just how is that Turtle managing to keep up?" he kept thinking.

Soon the finish line was in sight and Brer Rabbit could see Brer Buzzard hovering overhead ready to announce the winner. But he didn't see Brer Turtle come out of the woods and hide behind the line!

"Gimme the money, Brer Buzzard! I won the race!" hollered Brer Rabbit and Miss Meadows and the girls began to laugh and laugh.

34

Then blow me if that Brer
Turtle didn't rise up on his
little hind legs and say, "If
you'll just give me time to
catch my breath, ladies and
gents, I think I'll just
pocket that money myself!"
And tying the purse around
his neck and before Brer
Rabbit could engage his
brain to talk, he skedaddled
off home without so much
as a backward glance!

36

From time to time all the animals would get together and try to enjoy each other's company. They would ignore the fact that they had had their disagreements and Brer Rabbit would make up his mind once and for all that he was going to quit his bad ways and cause no more trouble around the neighbourhood.

But sooner or later the time would come when Brer Rabbit began to feel kind of twitchy. The more

contented and placid the
other animals seemed to
be, the more bad-tempered
and restless he became.

As the days rolled peacefully by, he lay in the long grass and kicked irritably at the buzzing gnats. He chewed peevishly at the melon stalks and scuffed his feet in the dust. He had a home and a full tummy but it seemed to him as if something was still missing.

One night after supper he was strolling around

wondering how to fill the hours before bedtime when he bumped into ole Brer Turtle. They shook hands solemnly.then sat down on the side of the road to chat. Pretty soon the talk came round to tales of the old days and how they hooted with laughter as the memories flooded back. Bye and bye Brer Rabbit gave a great sigh.

"I gotta confession to make, Brer Turtle," said he. "I miss those good ole, bad ole days."

Brer Turtle scratched his jaw gloomily. "Know just what you mean, Brer Rabbit," said he. "We sure had some fun back then."

"I gotta mighty strong urge to have some fun again, Brer Turtle," said Brer Rabbit meaningfully.

"I got that urge too, Brer Rabbit," replied Brer Turtle and soon they were happily hatching a plot.

"In the morning I'll go see Brer Fox, Brer Wolf and Brer Bear," announced Brer Rabbit. "I'll invite them to meet us down at the millpond tomorrow evening and we'll have a little fishing frolic. I'll do al the talking and you just say yes'!" Brer Turtle chortled with glee. "Happy to oblige, Brer Rabbit," he said. "Happy to oblige."

Brer Rabbit sauntered off home feeling cheerful, relaxed and more at peace with the world than he had done for weeks.

The next day he sent word of the fishing party to Brer Fox, Brer Wolf and Brer Bear and they were thrilled.

"What a fine idea!" said
Brer Fox, clasping his paws
under his chin.

"Now why didn't I think
of that!" said Brer Wolf
admiringly.

Hiding a sly grin, Brer
Rabbit loped off to Miss
Meadows' house and invited
her and the girls to join
them. So it was that they all
met up on the edge of the
millpond later that night.

Brer Bear carried a landing net, Brer Fox had a hook and line and Brer Turtle held a large box of wriggling maggots to use as bait.

Brer Turtle took great delight in shaking the box at Miss Meadows and the girls as they squealed with horror. "I'm gonna fish for mud-cats," said Brer Bear. "And I'm gonna fish for horneyheads," decided Brer Wolf. Brer Fox smiled kinda slow and winked at Brer Turtle. "Reckon I'm gonna catch me some suckers," he said quietly. With that he prepared to cast his hook into the water. Suddenly he started and the eyes nearly popped out of his head. He clutched his pole and scratched his head in bewilderment as he stared down into the depths of the pond. The girls grew uneasy and presently Miss Meadows called out, "Lawks, Brer Rabbit, just what have you seen in there?"

Brer Rabbit rubbed his chin and stared hard at the pond. Miss Meadows nervously gathered up her skirts. "I'm most monstrous scared of snakes," she quavered. "Tell me it ain't snakes, Brer Rabbit!" Brer Rabbit shook his head and sighed. "Well," he said, "we might all just as well turn around and go home for there'll be no fishing tonight.

Then Brer Turtle scrambled to the edge of the pond and peered over. He shook his head. "Well I never!" he said, most astonished. "Lawks a mercy!"

"Now don't be scared, ladies," reassured Brer Rabbit as he laid a comforting paw on Miss Meadows' arm. "Accidents will happen come what may and there's nothing at

ll for you to worry about."
Miss Meadows looked very
worried. "There has been
something of a mishap and
I'm very much afraid that
the moon has gone and
fallen in the water."

Everyone rushed to the
water's edge and looked in
and sure enough, there lay
the moon quivering at the
bottom of the pool.

"Well, well," said Brer Fox.

"Mighty bad, mighty bad," sighed Brer Wolf.

"Tut, tut, tut," tutted Brer Bear. Then the ladies looked in and Miss Meadows squawked, "Ain't that just too much?" Brer Rabbit shrugged his shoulders and spoke. "Well, you can all hum and haw but unless we get that moon out of the pond, there'll be no fishing for any of us tonight."

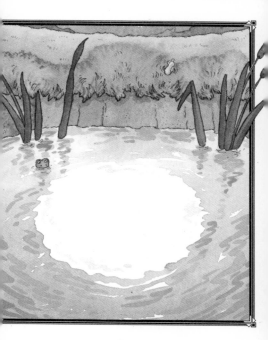

Brer Rabbit winked at Brer Turtle. "And if you don't believe me," he added, "you can just ask Brer Turtle."

"It's true sure enough," agreed Brer Turtle, nodding his head energetically. The animals decided at once that there was nothing for it but to take that moon from out of the pond.

"But how shall we do it?" asked Brer Bear. Then Brer

Rabbit closed his eyes tight and pretended to think hard. "I reckon the best way out of this here difficulty is to run round to ole Mr Mud Turtle and borrow his large fishing net. We're gonna have to drag that moon from the pond."

"Mr Mud Turtle is a close relation of mine," added Brer Turtle. "Fact is, I call him Unc Muck!"

So Brer Rabbit ran off to fetch the net and Brer Turtle filled the time by telling everyone that he believed this sort of thing had happened before and he had heard tell that if someone succeeded in pulling the moon out of a pond then they would also pull out a pot full of money at the same time.

Then Brer Bear, Brer Fox

and Brer Wolf grew mighty excited. "Seeing as how Brer Rabbit's been so good as to run and fetch the net, we'll do the job of hauling the moon from the water," said Brer Fox hastily.

So they all three waded into the pond and Brer Fox took hold of one end of the net, Brer Wolf took hold of the other, and Brer Bear followed behind.

They dragged the net
through the water and
hauled it up. No moon!
They made another haul.
Still no moon!

Soon they were right out in the middle of the pond and here the water was deep and cold. It ran in Brer Fox's ears and he shook his head. It ran in Brer Wolf's nose and he snorted. It ran in Brer Bear's mouth and he choked. They were so busy that they didn't notice the pond bottom suddenly dropped away from under their feet!

One by one their heads disappeared and bobbed up again as the poor animals thrashed the water with

their arms. They flailed
about so much it was a
wonder they didn't empty
the pond of all its water!

Soon they reached the
bank and you never saw
such poor bedraggled
creatures in all your life!

Miss Meadows and the girls tried to hide their snickering but they didn't make a very good job of it.

Brer Turtle was crying with laughter so bad that he had to pretend he had a fly in his eye so as not to cause offence.

Brer Rabbit gallantly helped Brer Bear, Fox and Wolf up onto dry land and slowly looked them up and down. "I think you better go home and get into some dry clothes, gentlemen," he said, acting all concerned. "Maybe we could try and catch the moon another night. You know, I'm sure you'll get lucky sooner or later because I hear tell that the moon will only bite the hook if you use fools as bait and I reckon that's the only way *you'll* catch her."

Brer Fox, Brer Bear and Brer Wolf looked at him blankly as the water dripped off their noses and they didn't see Brer Rabbit wink at Brer Turtle, or Brer Turtle wink back at him!

One day Brer Wolf was on his way home after a good day's fishing. He sauntered along with a string of fish over his shoulder when all of a sudden Miss Partridge flew out of the bushes right in front of his nose. She squawked so angrily that Brer Wolf figured she must be trying to lure him away from her nest of young 'uns.

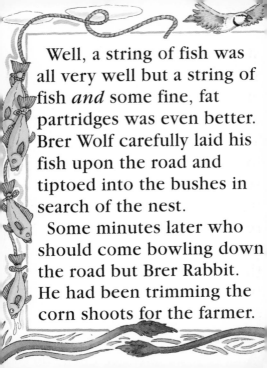

Well, a string of fish was
all very well but a string of
fish *and* some fine, fat
partridges was even better.
Brer Wolf carefully laid his
fish upon the road and
tiptoed into the bushes in
search of the nest.

Some minutes later who
should come bowling down
the road but Brer Rabbit.
He had been trimming the
corn shoots for the farmer.

Well, that's they way he saw it, anyway, even if the farmer didn't. He stopped and looked at the fishes. The fishes looked up at him ('cept they were dead so they couldn't really see him). Well, no self-respecting rabbit would have left the fishes lying there and Brer Rabbit wasn't about to make an exception, no, sirree.

Off he ran with the fishes over his shoulder and when Brer Wolf returned there was nothing on the ground but a fishy-smelling damp patch.

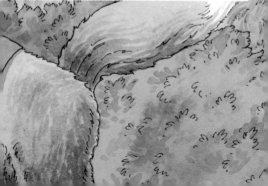

Brer Wolf pretty soon
worked out what had
happened. It could be no-
one else but that pesky Brer
Rabbit! But when he got to
Brer Rabbit's house and put
the matter to him, Brer
Rabbit flatly denied it. Brer
Wolf insisted. Brer Rabbit
disagreed. Brer Wolf
persisted. Brer Rabbit
protested. At last Brer
Rabbit looked him in the eye.

"If you're so sure I've got your fishes," he said, "well, you can just go out the back and kill my best cow." Now Brer Rabbit was sure that this would put an end to the matter. Nobody would make a generous offer like that if they were lying! But to his dismay, Brer Wolf took him at his word and off he skedaddled round the side of the house

n search of Brer Rabbit's
best cow. Wasn't long
before he found her and he
killed her on the spot.

Brer Rabbit was mighty
sore to see his plan backfire
but he wasn't beaten yet.

"Don't you worry, you
rabs," he told his wide-eyed
children. "Ain't nobody
going to take that meat
away from us." Then he had
an idea.

Brer Wolf had been arrested by the police some days earlier and ever since had been greatly afraid of a repeat performance.

"Police! It's the police, Brer Wolf!" cried Brer Rabbit at the top of his voice. "You better run and hide and I'll stay here and look after the cow until you get back." Well, you couldn't see Brer Wolf for dust.

Quickly Brer Rabbit set to work. He skinned the cow and salted the hide. He cut the meat into pieces and all his little children happily stowed it away in the smoke-house.

Then Brer Rabbit took the cow's tail and stuck one end in the ground. He allowed himself a quick chortle at the sight of it then wiped the smile of his face and called out loudly.

"The police have gone, Brer Wolf," he cried. "But you better come quick! Something strange is happening here. Your cow is going under the ground!"

Out from the bushes ran Brer Wolf and his jaw sagged as he beheld the scene before him. There stood Brer Rabbit gripping on to the end of the cow's tail as if his very life depended on it.

"Give me a hand, Brer Wolf!" he cried, kind of panic-stricken. "This here cow is trying to get deeper underground!"

Brer Wolf grabbed hold of the tail and pulled with all his might. He pulled and pulled and then — pop! — out came the tail from the ground!

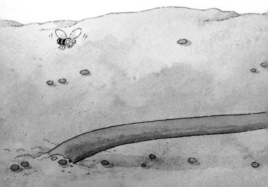

With a yelp, poor Brer Wolf landed flat on his you-know-what. He looked at the tail in his hand and he looked at the hole in the ground.

"Now look what you've been and gone and done," tutted Brer Rabbit. "You've pulled the tail right off the cow and I'll bet you can be pretty sure that cow is gone for good." But Brer

Wolf would not give up hope. He had been so close to eating that meat he could almost taste it and if the cow was within reach, he would have her for sure. Soon he was hard at work with a spade and the hole grew bigger and bigger. With each blow of his pickaxe and each shovelful of clay he felt sure he was getting closer.

Brer Rabbit sat back in his rocking chair and smiled happily as his children frolicked around him.

"He diggy, diggy, diggy, but no meat there!" he laughed. "He diggy, diggy, diggy, but no meat there!"

Joel Chandler Harris

The *Brer Rabbit* stories began as American
Negro fables, told by the slaves working on
plantations in the deep South of North America,
and almost certainly African in origin.
Joel Chandler Harris (1848-1908) insisted that
he did no more than simply retell the
stories, but in fact he showed great storytelling
skill in padding out what was often little more
than a folk saying. He also retained the
wonderfully rich dialect of the southern Negro
slaves, writing the words just as they would
have been said. This text has been adapted for
easier reading and understanding, but still
retains the flavour of Uncle Remus's relaxed
storytelling style.